Three Cheers for
TACKY

Helen Lester

Illustrated by Lynn Munsinger

MACMILLAN CHILDREN'S BOOKS

For my Aunt Betsy
– H.L.

Text copyright © 1994 Helen Lester
Illustrations copyright © 1994 Lynn Munsinger

First published in the USA in 1994 by Houghton Mifflin.

First published in Great Britain in 1996 by Macmillan Children's Books,
a division of Macmillan Publishers Limited,
25 Eccleston Place, London SW1W 9NF,
and Basingstoke.
Associated companies throughout the world.

ISBN 0 333 64130 2 HB
ISBN 0 333 65374 2 PB

1 3 5 7 9 8 6 4 2

A CIP catalogue record for this book is available
from the British Library.

Printed in Hong Kong

There once lived a group of penguins in a nice icy land.

One was Goodly, one was Lovely, one was Angel, one was Neatly, one was Perfect.

And one was Tacky.

Tacky was the odd bird.

When they grew old enough, Goodly, Lovely, Angel, Neatly, Perfect and Tacky went to school.

They read books.

They wrote their names.

They learned their numbers.

GREAT
PENGUIN
CHEERING
CONTEST

ALL [illegible]
[illegible] PRIZE

One day at school the penguins noticed a sign with an
exciting announcement: their class had been invited
to take part in a great Penguin Cheering Contest.
Penguin classes from all over the iceberg would
be there and the team with the finest cheer would
win shiny blue bow ties.

Imagine what they could do with shiny blue bow ties!

Right after school, Goodly, Lovely, Angel, Neatly and Perfect
hurried away to practise their cheer.

Softly and properly they began:

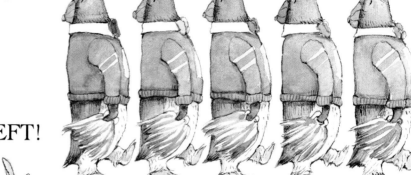

1, 2, 3, LEFT!

1, 2, 3, RIGHT!

Stand up!

Sit down!

Say "Good night"!

They did it beautifully, even the first time through.

Then up waddled Tacky, a little late.
And a little loud.
"What's happening?" he blared.
"We're practising our cheer, that's what's
happening," they replied.
   1, 2, 3, LEFT!
   1, 2, 3, RIGHT!
   Stand up!
   Sit down!
   Say "Good night"!

Tacky gave it a try.

1, 2, 3, LEFT!

A, B, C, RIGHT!

Flop down!

Roll over!

Say, what's for supper?

"Tacky," they said patiently, "we are a team, and if you are on the team you must be exactly like the rest of us."

He wanted very much to be on the team,
so Tacky tried to cooperate and move with a stiff upper
beak like the rest of them.
But how could he see where he was going with a stiff
upper beak in the way?

And directions were not always easy.

1, 2, 3, LEFT!
1, 2, 3, LEFT!
1, 2, 3, LEFT!
1, 2, 3, LEFT!
"Where is everybody?" he wondered.

Tacky had trouble coming up
with the proper costume.

And his pompoms were never quite right.

Would this team ever have
the chance to win
the shiny blue bow ties?

The penguins practised and practised and practised and practised until finally, the day before the contest,

1, 2, 3, LEFT!
1, 2, 3, RIGHT!
Stand up!

Sit down!
Say "Good night"!
TACKY GOT IT RIGHT!

The next morning teams from all over the iceberg
gathered for the great Penguin Cheering Contest.
Each team waited nervously to perform.
But no team was more nervous than Tacky's.
Could he do it right, just one more time?

The first team marched on stage.

    PIP, PIP, PIP.

    PIP, PIP, PIP.

    PIP, PIP, PIP.

       Rah. And the judges looked bored.

Another team marched forth.
1 – 2 – 3 – 4 – 5 – 6 – 7 – 8 – 9 – 10 – Sis – boom – bah,
and backed off, 10 – 9 – 8 – 7 – 6 – 5 – 4 – 3 – 2 – 1.
And the judges yawned.

A third team chanted,
    Wave the pompom,
    Hold it high,
    Bow politely,
    Say "Good-bye"! And the judges snored.

Finally there was only one team left – Tacky's.
With quivering beaks they faced the sleeping audience
and the snoring judges.
This was it.

Goodly, Lovely, Angel, Neatly, Perfect and Tacky began.
1, 2, 3, OH FOR CRYING OUT LOUD!

The audience gasped, startled by Tacky's loud voice.
The odd bird had tripped over the tails of his
Hawaiian shirt and crashed belly-down.

His horrified team mates carried on,
  1, 2, 3, RIGHT!

Poor Tacky, now a bit muddled, pulled his sweater over his head.
The sight of a headless penguin got the whole crowd laughing.

Stand up!
Sit down!
Say "Good night"!

By now the crowd was on its feet begging for more.
"Bravo!" "That was great!" "Another cheer!"

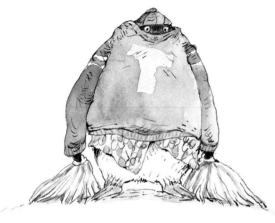

Tacky poked his head out.
Another cheer?
Well, if they insisted.
He gave them a second cheer.

1, 2, 3, LEFT!

A, B, C, RIGHT!

Flop down!

Roll over!

Say, what's for supper?

The crowd roared, the judges slapped each other on the back
and even the other penguin teams clapped wildly.

So Tacky led everyone in a third cheer!

1, 2, 3, YAY!
Rooty toot toot HOORAY!
High Flippers!
High Flippers!
We're okay!

Penguins everywhere gave high flippers.

There was no question who wore the shiny blue bow ties home.
Tacky was an odd bird, but a nice bird to have around.